HI AND LOIS captures those tender, silly, helpful, ridiculous, sad, humorous, outrageous, cozy, intimate, secure, frustrating, unnerving moments experienced by many a suburban family member. The accuracy of these portrayals frequently must spark flashes of recognition among the 45 million people who read HI AND LOIS in the 800 newspapers which feature it.

The success of the strip is a tribute to its creators—Mort Walker and Dik Browne—who know whereof they write, for they are both suburbanites and fathers (Mort has seven children, Dik three).

The success of the strip may also be proof that the home is still the richest vein of human comedy and possibly the most appealing. As Mort (seven children) puts it: "My best research walks in and out of my studio all day borrowing pencils and papers!"

Hi and Lois Books by Mort Walker and Dik Browne

HI AND LOIS: AMERICAN GOTHIC
HI AND LOIS: THE BRIGHT STUFF
HI AND LOIS: FATHER FIGURE
HI AND LOIS: MAMA'S HOME

Hi and Lois

THE BRIGHT STUFF

BY MORT WALKER and DIK BROWNE

CHARTER BOOKS, NEW YORK

HI AND LOIS: THE BRIGHT STUFF

A Charter Book / published by arrangement with
King Features Syndicate, Inc.

PRINTING HISTORY
Charter Original / June 1984

All rights reserved.
Copyright © 1982, 1983, 1984 by King Features Syndicate, Inc.
This book may not be reproduced in whole or in part,
by mimeograph or any other means, without permission.
For information address: The Berkley Publishing Group,
200 Madison Avenue, New York, New York 10016.

ISBN: 0-441-32899-7

Charter Books are published by The Berkley Publishing Group,
200 Madison Avenue, New York, New York 10016.
PRINTED IN THE UNITED STATES OF AMERICA